4RM
A Collection of Short Stories

Compiled and edited for print
by RM Morrissey

Written by students for students

First Published 2022 by RM Morrissey

ISBN: 9798837470486
Copyright © RM Morrissey, 2022

To all the hard-working students and teachers who make writing happen.

Foreword

Dear reader,

In this book, you will find a collection of different and unique stories written by our year four students this year. Our inspiration for the stories told within was the idea of being a fish out of water. Something being somewhere that it doesn't belong.

This year we studied The Wild Robot by Peter Brown and were inspired to write out own stories about someone who ends up in the wrong place and because of this, has to figure out how to survive or how to get back home.

All of our students worked hard and enjoyed writing their short stories. For many of them, this will be the first time that they have been able to type up their stories and for all of them, the first time they will see their story published in print. It it my hope that seeing their stories published will inspire them as writers and give some of them the confidence to pursue their passions in writing, building on their imaginations and developing their writing skills.

It has been a pleasure reading and editing these stories for print. I hope you enjoy reading them as much as I did.

RM Morrissey

A Human on Top of the Bed!

By: RM Morrissey

This story starts at midnight. Not a minute before and not a minute after. You see, the portal only opens once every night at exactly the stroke of midnight and closes very soon after.

What portal, you ask? Well, the one which allows the monsters under the bed to come out, of course! And Jenkin's bedroom was the perfect bedroom for monsters because it was a mess and monsters... well, they love dirty, messy, nasty things. They love the scattered piles of dirty laundry. They love the mounds of snotty tissues whenever Jenkins has a cold. And they love all the other random nasties that are littered here, there and everywhere.

"Sniff, sniff! Ooo, that's the smell of toe clippings, Mama!

Real nasty, tasty ones! And that! That smell is of dirty socks, Mama! Ooo, can I have a dirty sock? Please, pretty please, Mama?"

This little one was named Goobie-Boogie-Dirty-Sniff-Socker Junior, but his mum just called him Gob for short. They were a family of Feetslickers, but you might know them simply as monsters from under the bed. They were small, about the size of a yappy dog. They were covered in fur, kind of like a yappy dog, and they had legs and ears and mouths, sort of like a yappy dog. But they certainly were not yappy dogs as they stood on two legs like humans and tried to be as quiet as can be so that they did not wake the owner of their soon to be dinner.

"Toe clippings covered in toe jam and smelly socks from sports day... Why Gob? We've stumbled upon some real treasure tonight. I'm sure that hooman won't care if we take a thing or two."

Now, monsters from under the bed don't really like to be called that because, according to them, they are very different. A Feetslicker would never be caught eating fingernails and an Armspitsniff would never dream of sniffing toes. You see, every different type of monster from under the bed, from Boogerslups to Lintbellies to Fartsrollers and Undiesnatchers, they all like to eat certain nasties from little children. And Feetslickers, they wanted socks!

Gob and his mum rummaged through all sorts of nasty

things, looking for the best, most delectable items for their dinner, and then they hurried off to get back under the bed before the portal closed. Gob's mum had her arms full of the smelliest, sweat-drenched, putrid socks she could find (the ones from sports day), and she scurried off through the portal back home without realising that she was missing one important thing. Her son! Gob was not with her. No, he found himself stuck face first, bottom up in a pile of laundry, diving for something tasty at the very bottom. He was so focused on the delightful stench that he didn't notice his mum was leaving. And she was so focused on her rumbling belly that she hadn't noticed he was missing.

By the time Gob realised what had happened, it was too late. He raced back to the portal with mouldy socks in his mouth, only to find that it had closed shut for the night. "Mama? Mama?! MAMA?!" Gob wailed when he realised he had been behind. He didn't know what to do and then he heard it - a noise that no monster ever wants to hear. It was coming from on top of the bed!

"Whah? Who's there? Is something under my bed?" It was Jenkins. The kid had woken up when Gob was screaming for his mum, and he was scared. He pulled his covers up to his eyes and tried to convince himself that he was dreaming. There were no such things as monsters under the bed.

Gob was paralysed with fear, like a deer caught in

headlights. He was so afraid he didn't even want to breathe. He needed to think. Where was he going to hide when the sun rose? Kids aren't afraid of monsters under the bed when the sun is up. If he didn't find a place to hide, who knows what will happen? What do children do to monsters? Do they eat them? Tickle them? Dress them up as pretty dolls? All of these things are a monster's worst nightmare!

Gob had an idea! He would hide in the sock drawer. Surely, this was the perfect place to hide!

Hours past, the sun rose and Jenkins yawned a ridiculously big yawn and Gob froze as still as he could at the back of the sock drawer. Gob whispered to himself, "What kind of terrifying hooman makes such a terrible noise? It sounds like the wailing of an elephant!" Then Gob slapped his hands over his mouth and stuffed that dirty sock in it. He forgot that he had to be quiet!

Jenkins was walking over to his drawers and Gob heard each and every thump. "Definitely like an elephant. Ohh, I want my mama!" he thought to himself as he tightened his hands around his mouth, trying to not even breathe. The drawer opened and Gob cowered at the back, ready to die from fear. But then, the drawer closed. Gob took a deep breath in and decided he needed to find a new place to hide. Someplace where Jenkins would never find him so that he could never lick him like a lollipop, or dip him into ketchup, or some other crazy thing that a human might do.

All of these things were a monster's worst nightmare!

Gob had an idea! While Jenkins was in the shower, he would hide in the closet! Surely, this was the perfect place to hide!

When Jenkins had finished in the shower, he came back into the room and he was singing. "That sounds like a dying cat. My ears! My ears! Ohh, I want my mama!" he thought to himself as he tried to stuff the dirty sock from his mouth into his ears. The horrible singing got closer and closer, and Gob squished his ears closed tighter and tighter and then the closet door opened!

Horrible thoughts raced around Gob's mind, "He's going to force me to attend tea parties in pink, frilly dresses and make me listen to that awful singing. I'd rather die. Goodbye Mama! I'm off to the land of smelly socks!" And then the closet door closed, and the singing faded. Gob took a deep breath, took the sock out of his ears, and decided that he needed to find a new place to hide. Someplace where Jenkins would never find him so that he could never make him wear clean shoes, or clean clothes, or make him take a bath! All of these things are a monster's worst nightmare!

Gob had an idea! While Jenkins was gone, doing whatever human boys do during the day, he would hide under the bed! Surely this was the perfect place to hide!

Gob hid under the bed for what seemed like forever, but really it was only about the length of a school day. And then he heard it. The sound of elephant stomps and the cries of a dying cat. Jenkins was home and Gob felt a shiver race down his back. He scooched to the very back of his hiding place and pulled that sock up to his face like a blanket that might protect him from that human child. And he waited, and waited, and waited, but the boy never came back into his room. "Where could that hooman be?" Gob whispered to himself. "I hear him, but I don't see him."

Hours passed and Gob lay hidden under that sock under the bed, unable to move, scared that at any moment Jenkins would return and find him and snatch him! Crazy thoughts ran through Gob's head about what the boy would do to him if he found him. Thoughts so scary, so crazy, so disturbing that they cannot be written down. All of these things are a monster's worst nightmare!

Then it happened. The sun had set, darkness crept in, and there was a thump, thump, thump as the boy returned to this room. He was muttering all the things which his mum had been telling him. "Jenkins, clean your room. Jenkins, pick up your dirty laundry. Jenkins, all your clothes are smelly." These things didn't seem so bad to Gob, but then he remembered he was hiding under a dirty sock!

Gob watched in horror from under his sock-blanket as Jenkins picked up all his dirty laundry and put it in the laundry hamper. Even his dirty PE clothes. There was nothing left on the ground... it was clean!

Then, Jenkins looked towards his bed and saw that there were clothes still under it that he had to clean up or his mum would not be impressed. He got down on his hands and knees and started tossing the items out. A dirty shirt with gravy stains, a pair of trousers that were clearly worn in the mud, and underwear that had been there for goodness knows how long. The only piece of dirty laundry left was the sock that Gob was hiding under. He reached for it, but his arms weren't quite long enough, so he laid down on the floor. He stretched, and stretched, and stretched, reaching for the last bit of laundry. Gob could only see what was happening through the small hole in the bottom of the sock.

Fingers crawled closer and closer and closer, and Gob's heart beat faster and faster and faster. And just when Gob was about to give up his hiding place and run for it, the hand stopped. Jenkins couldn't reach any further. "Oh well. If I can't reach it, surely mum will never notice it. She said clean up my floor. She didn't reeeally say clean up under the bed! That can wait until tomorrow."

Gob was safe, the boy couldn't reach. Clearly, this was the perfect place to hide. And hide Gob did. He stayed hidden under the bed while Jenkins got ready for bed. He stayed hidden under the bed when the boy's mum came to read him a story and kiss him good night. He stayed hidden under the bed when Jenkins finally fell asleep and started snoring like a pig.

He stayed hidden until midnight. Not a minute before and not a minute after, for the portal only opens once every night at exactly the stroke of midnight and closes very soon after. Gob knew this and so do you. And so did Gob's mum. The second the clock struck midnight, she burst through the portal looking for her son and there, under a mouldy sock, he was snoring like a pig. She picked him up, told him how much she missed him, and gave him a kiss good night as they went through the portal back to their world.

A Journey Through the Forgotten Land

By Aidan

This story begins in the Arctic, where a young penguin was growing. The hatchling's name was James, and he roamed free whenever he wanted and had a talent for swimming. He had the perfect life, but then, at the age of 13, an incident occurred which left him emotionally scarred for life.

The incident happened on March 19th 3046. It was a wonderful day to be alive because the sun was out and a cool breeze flew past you every now and then. But then, as the penguins were enjoying the spring life, a vortex opened nearby and a terrible storm came with it.

"Umm, guys? I think we should go inside now..." James said, trembling at the sight of the storm.

BOOM! Then it happened. Lightning struck and it took the lives of James's parents. James stood there, still, shocked and silent like a scared deer caught in headlights as his friends cowered away in fear.

The storm took their lives too. James, heartbroken, stood there with nothing left. And then, in the midst of his loss, he was lifted off the ground and his world went black.

James woke up only to realize the he was nowhere near home. He was stuck in an oak tree's branches!

"Oh no no! Where in the world am I?!" James thought to himself. Anyone could tell he was panicking.

James took a deep breath and wiggled his way out of the tree's grasp and observed his surroundings. He could see the lush, soft grass dancing in the wind as a pale, round moon shone over. He could hear a stream flowing into the ocean, the chitter of insects and the hooting of owls, as well as the cries of small forest mammals.

James knew this was where his journey would begin. He waddled through the forest, knowing that he could not go back home. He exited the forest which led to an abandoned city that nature had claimed for themselves.

"Woah ... this is crazy!" James said, admiring the night sky.

Then James saw a star on the ground. It was large, yellow and it sparkled. James tried to pick it up, but then, with James on it, the star decided it wanted to float. But this was not the case at all. After a bit of fiddling with it, James realized he could control the star using his mind.

"Left!" James thought. The star followed his exact command.

"Right!" James thought. Again, the star followed his exact command.

"Forwards!" James thought. Once again, the star followed his exact command.

James used his new-found power to find a lake. Because he was hungry. Really hungry. Seeing a penguin fly down to a lake was an unusual sight as penguins are, of course, flightless birds. But then James splashed into the water and he had a realization: what if he ate his star? He needed to know.

James opened his mouth wider than ever before and gobbled up his star. It was actually quite tasty and something happened, to James's surprise. He was now glowing rainbow colours and he had a star wand in his hand. And for no reason whatsoever, he knew what it could do. He waved his wand and a vortex opened, just like the one from the day before. James knew what he had to do. He jumped in and his world went black.

He was back at home.

"Well, maybe I was wrong about not being able to go back home."

The Missing Girl

By: Ariana

This story starts in a beautiful home with a nice family who lived inside. They had a daughter named Pheobe and she was a nice girl. She mostly spent her time reading or helping people and everyone thought that she was the perfect child.

In the morning, Pheobe went to the garden and she saw a beautiful butterfly. She started to chase it but she wasn't paying attention and she didn't realise how far she was from her home.

After a while, Pheobe looked up and saw that it was dark. "How is it dark? It was just morning. I'm so confused." She turned around but she didn't know where she was. She didn't recognise it. All she knew was that she was very, very far away from where she should be.

It was dark so she had to make a decision. She decided that she should start gathering wood for a fire so she could see. But as she was collecting wood she tripped over a rock and as she was getting up, she saw a beautiful little cottage.

In the cottage, she saw a lady feeding a hungry cat some fish so she thought it was safe. She went to the lady and asked her if she can stay with her for the night and the lady the lady said that she could.

When Pheobe's parents found out that she was missing they told the servants to look for her. They searched high and low, near and far, but they couldn't find her anywhere. It was like she vanished into thin air. They returned to Phoebe's parents to tell her the news and her parents burst into tears thinking that something terrible had happened.

The next day, Pheobe went downstairs in the cottage and she found the lady making breakfast. Phoebe was so happy as she hadn't eaten since yesterday morning. The old lady offered her some food. As they were eating, Pheobe asked, "What is your name?"

"Emily is my name, little one."

Pheobe asked Emily if she could help her find her home and Emily agreed. They started to search and eventually things started to look familiar. After a while, Pheobe noticed a beautiful garden and she remembered that it was hers!

She then ran inside her home and hugged her parents, and her parents were shocked to see her. After she had given them both huge hugs, she explained what happened to her yesterday. Her parents were so happy that Emily had taken care of their daughter that she was given a huge bonus for finding her.

Emily returned quietly to her cottage and Pheobe never chased after butterflies again.

The Missing Kitten!

By: Aya

This story begins in a beautiful home with a kitten named Nina who was the sweetest kitten ever. Though, sometimes she knocks off some paintings and books off the shelves, but no one seemed to mind because she was so sweet.

The cat was normally at home, but something had happened! She was missing!

The cat's owner, Valentina, called for her mum. "Mummy!"

Her mum answered, "Yes, sweetie?"

"Where's Nina?"

"I actually don't know. Hmmm, let's check!"

Valentina and her mum went upstairs. "Is she in the

attic?" her mum said to her.

"No, she's not here," Valentina said.

So they went to Valentina's room. "Is she in your room?" mum asked her daughter?

"No, she's not in my room," Valentina said.

Valentina and her mum kept searching for Nina and they never gave up because Valentina always spent fun times with Nina. They read books, did drawing together and Valentina's favourite parts were watching Nina eat and getting to feed Nina treats!

While Valentina was looking for Nina, she realised that her mum had gone to take a nap.

Zzzz Zzzzz Zzzzz

"Ugh, never mind! I will find Nina myself. Oh wait on a minute! She's always in her bush outside! Let's check there!" Valentina went outside and looked in the bush.

"Yay! Oh, wait … that's her toy. Ugh I will never find Nina." Valentina walked around her back garden sadly. "Meow, meow, meow," trying to talk to her cat.

Then, she had an idea! "Oh, wait! I've got a picture of Nina. I can print it and tape it to every single wall in town. Someone is bound to help me find her!"

So Valentina taped up posters all over the city so that everyone could see that Nina was missing.

Valentina was sitting on a bench and she saw a strange looking creature look at her sign. "Is that an alien," Valentina thought to herself. "No, it can't be …"

Then, all of a suddenly she just teleported to Mars. "Huh! Where am I?"

"Beep boop blee pop bingo!" said a strange looking alien similar to the one that was looking at her sign back in the city.

Valentina had no idea what he just said, but she did recognise that he was pointing to a field filled with craters, so she went to look. She looked in every crater on Mars. She looked at the ones on the bottom, the ones in the middle and the ones on the top. And there she was, Nina!

"NINAAAAAAAAAAAAA! HOW DID YOU GET HERE?!"

"Meow, meeeeow, meooow!" the cat said, jumping into Valentina's arms.

"So wait, if you're here and I'm here … how do we get back? We're stuck here I think, Nina!"

The End

The Doughnut and the Pizza

By: Zara

Once a upon a time there was a girl that wanted a doughnut. So she went to the shop, when she was there, she saw a ton of doughnuts. But she had to pick one, so she picked the chocolate sugar doughnut.

"Oh, I can't believe there are so many doughnuts here, my mouth is watering," said the girl

The girl paid for the doughnut and put it in her bag. After a while she wanted pizza. So she went to the pizza shop when she stepped into the pizza shop she saw pizza .The doughnut got scared and was like

"What if the pizza eats me? Ahhhh!"

The girl asked for a cheese pizza when she got it she took the doughnut out and put the pizza in. Then the girl left. The doughnut got scared and was scared.

After a while with the doughnut in the pizza shop pizza were getting sold and the doughnut got more us to the place. In a while it got dark and all of the pizza were getting sold it got darker and darker and darker! All of a sudden it got dark and the doughnut was the only one there.

"Why is everything got dark?" said the doughnut.

All of a sudden it became morning and there was more pizza the doughnut was moving left to right, but he couldn't because the pizza was too heavy. The pizza next to him was staring weirdly.

At that day after a while the girl came back and found her doughnut so she asked the man and said can I take my doughnut, so the girl took the doughnut and after a second, poof! The doughnut was in her tummy.

A few hours later the girl had a tummy ache. So the girl went home when she got home she was felling something in her tummy moving she wondered why she thought that she ate to much but what was actually happening was that the doughnut in her tummy was fighting with the pizza inside her tummy.

The pizza punched the doughnut and the sugar sprinkles fell off. But then, the doughnut punched the pizza and all of the cheese fell off.

The girl felt even more pain so she decided to go to the doctors. When she reached there, she said "My tummy hurts really bad it feels like someone is kicking!"

The doctor checked her tummy and found the doughnut and pizza and she threw them and went home feeling better!

The End!

Out of this World

By: Kiranjeet

5 … 4 … 3 … 2 … 1… blastoff and straight towards Mars.

A half hour later and they were almost there but they only had a little bit of fuel left. Despite that, they landed successfully on Mars. They looked that the fuel tank and there was one one percent fuel remaining. It takes about a month to refuel so that astronaut was stuck here for at least that long. And then, the astronaut saw something. Something green and glowy and bright!

He went towards the light and knocked on the door of the building. He knocked and then ran away to the side of it. When he touched the green, glowy thing, it was acid that burned through their gloves. The door opened and there were aliens that came out.

24

"Oh my god! Ah! Ah! Ahhhhhhhh!" the astronaut screamed as they sprinted back to their spaceship. They waited a full say, and then they went back and knocked on the same door, but they didn't run to the side this time. The door opened.

"Hello," he said tot he aliens that opened the door.

"Hello, there. You will be good for dinner. Err … I mean, come inside! It is a little dark outside."

The astronaut wasn't too sure, but the alien was right. It was getting dark outside so he went in.

"Have some food," one of the aliens said with an evil look on their face.

"Umm, no thanks," the astronaut replied.

"Come on, it is so hard to make and tastes so fine."

The astronaut took a sip. "Yum! Can I have some more?"

The aliens gave him more and then his fingers started to melt. Then his body started to melt. He was nothing but a puddle of goo.

The rocket ship took a whole month to refuel itself, but its pilot never returned to take it back to Earth.

The Poor Cat

By: Falak

Chapter 1

My story starts at midnight. There was a cat that did not have a home and lived on the road with trash. She did not have any one to take care of her so one time, when she was tried of living on the street, she went out of the trash and tried to find a home.

As she was looking for a new home, she got sleepier and sleepier. Then she saw somewhere that might have been a good place to live, so she went to. A strange house.

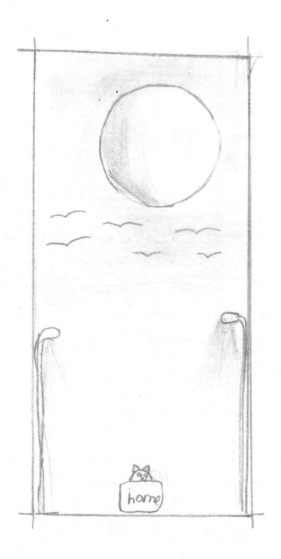

Chapter 2

When she got to the house, the door was open, but she didn't really know where she was because her eyes were closed from being so sleepy. She couldn't stand anymore so she fell on the pillows and had a nice sleep.

Morning came, so she woke up, and was hungry so she went to look for cat food. She did not know where in this house she could find any cat food. She didn't know in which room she should look in first. So she went in every room.

After a few minutes, only one room was left to go, so she went in that room too and finally, she found cat food. As she was eating, the whole house started to move and then the cat tried to run away from the house but she couldn't and then something went so strange.

Chapter 3

Then the cat eventually opened the door because the room stopped moving. When the cat opened the door, she was not on Earth. She was on Mars. It was also dark and the cat was scared. She went back into the house because she was scared and went to find a room to hide in. The room she found was incredibly dirty. There were dirty clothes and socks all over the floor.

The cat didn't want to hide in a dirty room because she didn't like the smell of dirty clothes. So, she looked around the room to find a clean place where she could hide. The only place that was clean in the entire room was in the closet, so she went in there and hid.

The next morning, when it was light out, the cat got out of the closet and went outside. It wasn't dark anymore so she wasn't afraid. There was no more food in the house, so she had to go looking on Mars to find some food. She looked everywhere and eventually found a box that had some food inside.

The cat tried to find a way home, but she couldn't ever find one so she decided to live on Mars.

The End

The Lost Princess and the Boy

By: Denisa

Bella was arguing with her parents, so Bella had an idea, she was going to run away from the castle. She took some normal clothes and put her hair in a bun and after that, she left. She was walking out of the castle, and then she started to run around for some fresh air but while doing this, accidentally bumped into someone.

She realized that it was a boy! She said, "Sorry."

But when she tried to run away, he held her hand tightly and said, "What's your name?"

Bella responded, "My name is Bella."

Jake said, "Your name is beautiful, Bella."

Bella said, "Thank you."

Bella asked, "Can I come and stay at your house?"

Jake replied,"Yes, but you're going to need to hide from my parents."

Jake thought it would be a good idea to hang out for the day at an amusement park. Bell thought that sounded like fun so they went. When they got there, Jake said, "First, let's go on a ride." Jake and Bella went on a roller coaster together.

Bella said, "I'm tired," so Jake went with Bella to his house.

Jake said, "If you want you can sleep on my bed. I'll sleep in my sleeping bag."

Bella said, "Thank you for letting me sleep in your bed." She yawned then fell asleep on Jake's bed.

The next day, Jake had to go to school, so he quickly made himself breakfast and also made Bella some. Then Bella woke up and saw that Jake was gone and that Jake made her breakfast. She also realized that Jake's parents were gone too so that meant that Bella was home alone.

Then Bella turned on the news while she was still eating. She heard them say that the princess ran away from the castle. Bella quickly turned off the TV and started to look around but didn't find anything interesting.

She was bored so she just went to Jake's school. When she arrived, she saw him sitting at the stands. Then Bella went up to him and said, "What's wrong?"

Jake replied with a sigh then Bella said, "What happened?"

Jake replied, "Someone keeps bullying me and everyday I have to do her homework. She's the principal's daughter and she get's whatever she wants. She used to pay me to do her homework but she stopped paying me and now forces me to do it for free."

Bella said, "Don't worry because I'm going to deal with it."

Jake said, "Ok."

Then Bella put on some black clothes she found on the ground. She went in the girls bathroom where the principal's daughter, Sarah, was. Bella went in the stall where Sarah was and Bella said, "Give me all your money or else!"

Sarah replied, "Why? You know that I'm the principal's daughter, right?"

Bella said, "Because if you don't, then I'm going to beat you up. And if you tell your little daddy about this, then there will be consequences!"

So Sarah listened to Bella and gave her all her money. Then Bella ran to Jake and showed him all of Sarah's money. Bella took off the black clothes and put them back on the ground. She and Jake ran all the way back to Jake's house. It was already night time when they got there and Bella and Jake both went to sleep.

The next day, again Jake had to go to school and his parents were gone too so that meant Bella was home alone once again. This time she went all across the Kingdom. She went to a cotton candy stand, got some cotton candy and went to a amusement park and she played some games and won two prizes! After that, Jake came back home.

Bella was sleeping and one of her prizes were with her and the other one was on Jake's sleeping bag. Jake just held onto the little bear and fell fast asleep.

The next day, Bella was so happy because Jake got to stay home today. Bella had a fun idea that she could do with Jake. She said, "Jake, let's go to the park and have a picnic."

Jake replied, "Ok, but we're going have to go get some food."

Bella said, "Don't worry because we're going to get some food and deserts on the way there."

Jake took a big red and white picnic blanket, picnic basket and took Bella's hand and ran all the way to the shop. They bought some food and deserts then they both ran all the way to the park.

Jake put the picnic blanket down on the ground and Bella took the food out of the picnic basket, and they both took a sandwich and ate it all up. Then, when they finished eating all the food, Jake took the deserts out of the picnic basket. They both took a slice of chocolate cake and once they finished eating the deserts, they ran all the way back to Jake's house. They were tired, so they curled up and went to bed.

The next day, Jake had to go to school once again so that

left Bella home alone once again. She looked around and this time she found something interesting! Jake's phone! She looked down and saw that someone was texting him and it said, "Where are the photos of the lost princess?" Then she saw photos that there were photos of Bella. Bella got so angry that she left Jake's house and went to the palace. When she got there, Bella's parents were so happy to see her.

It was the royal dance and Bella saw the prince that her parents wanted her to marry.

"He isn't that bad," said Bella.

Then Jake burst through the castle doors and said to Bella, "What happened? Why are you here?"

Bella replied,"I can't believe that you were going to sell some pictures of me!"

Jake said, "I'm sorry, I needed the money because my mum is really sick. But I didn't show her the pictures of you. I knew it was wrong so I came here to apologize and to tell you that ... I like you!"

Then Bella said, "I like you too and I forgive you. Also, don't worry about your mum because I'll pay for the hospital bill and for the surgery."

Jake replied, "Oh my gosh! Thank you so much! You're the best!"

Jake asked, "Do you want to dance with me, princess?"

Then Bella replied, "Of course!"

Bella and Jake dance with each other at the royal ball and

her parents let her marry Jake instead of that snobby prince!

The Monster is Trapped in a Crazy Child's Bedroom

By: Fatmata

Our story begins with a monster that is trapped in a crazy child's bedroom.

Part 1

Once upon a time, there was a monster in a crazy child's bedroom. The monster was wondering how he got in a crazy child's bedroom. She was sleeping but, she heard footsteps, so she hid in a underwear drawer.

"Ew! This is so smelly and stinky. When did this child wash her underwear?" The monster complained.

The crazy child's name is Beep-Boop-Pee-Poo Jr. but her mom just want to call her Chicky.

"Chicky, come downstairs, you have school today and you are going to be late for school!" Her mother scolded.

"Mommy! Leave me alone, just give me one more hour to sleep pleeeease!"

"CHICKY! Stop being a spoiled, little brat! Just come to the kitchen ... NOW!"

"Fine, mommy." Chicky said as she lazily got out of bed and started to get ready for school.

"Geez, this child is literally crazy." The monster said, hiding inside the underwear drawer. "If I behaved like that, my mommy would surely eat me!"

Part 2

The child opened her underwear drawer and she saw the monster.

"Hey! What are you doing here? How do you know my address?" Chicky said to the monster with her hands on her hips. She clearly wasn't afraid of a monster in her drawers!

"Umm, I don't know I just teleported here," the monster said as it back further into the drawer. "Umm, shouldn't you be afraid of me? I'm a monster after all!"

Chicky had a big grin on her face, "Ha-ha-ha! Your're mine now."

38

Part 3

Chicky was a bit of a crazy child and she didn't want this monster scaring any other children so she pushed the monster in a cold fridge. She left the monster there until the monster was dead. Or at least she though that he was dead ...

Without showing any fear at all, Chicky said to her mom, "Coming mommy."

"What took you so long, Chicky?"

"Nothing, mommy."

The monster was so strong that he broke out of the fridge, and he ran fast as he could to get back to monster land with other monsters to live happily ever.

Chicky got home after school and checked on the monster, but the fridge was empty. She didn't like that so she set a trap for that night. Next time the monster shows up, she'd be ready and that monster wouldn't escape a second time!

Escape From the Zoo

By: Gideon

This story, it starts a midnight. They are escaping from he zoo to find their parents. Who you ask? Well, the spider, the frog, the cat, ant their leader, and the snake of course!

The animals all lived in the wild. But one day when the animals were babies, the most evil animal took them to the zoo for display, the all mighty, baby scorpion.

So now, let me tell you about the animals. First, Gary. Gary's parents got him anything he wanted, like anything he wanted. And now Theo. Theo and his parents always got the most bugs in their spider webs. It was always a competition for that webby family. After Theo, we have Lila. Lila and her parents always went out to find something to eat. And the last of them Lilly. Lilly's parents always taught her how to slither like a pro.

As they were escaping, they had to get over water and since Lila could run on water, it had to be her to help the others. They all jumped on her and ZOOM! They were long gone across the water.

The animals saw a shark and they screamed. "AHHHHHHH!"

The shark wasn't dangerous or harmful, he was a part of a secret agency that helps animals find their parents whom they were taken away from. The shark said to them, "There were some parents at the agency a few days ago looking for their children. We said that we would try and find them."

"Maybe," said Lilly, "Can you tell us where the location to the headquarters is?"

The shark replied, "Yes, of course I can tell you that! You have to go to the island over there and then you have to go through the sewer door. After that, you will see some spiders that will lead you to a school in the sewers. And from there, the frog at the school will tell you what to do next."

The animals started to leave, but the shark called them back. "Don't forget to tell them that mission control sent you so that they know that I helped you."

Lily asked the shark, "Hey, can you give us a ride to the island? Lila is getting a bit tired with all of us on her back."

"Sure! Hop on!" the shark told them.

The shark took them to the island and they hopped off. They ran quickly to find the sewer door and finally they found it under a bunch of vines and rubbish. But the door wouldn't open. Lily remembered that the shark wanted them to say mission control, so they tried that as a password and the door creaked open.

They went into the sewer and traveled for about a half hour until they came upon the spider that the shark told them about.

The spider was there and Lily said to him, "The shark sent us to you. Can you take us to the school?"

The spider said, "Certainly I can take you there." They traveled through the twists and turns of the sewers until they came upon a rat. The rat didn't like other animals near its home so it growled at them and tried to chase them away. The spider spun a web and caught the rat before it could hurt the animals.

After they were safe, they carried on their journey and eventually arrived at the school.

The spider told them that the frog would take care of them from here and he left.

The frog popped out of a pond and Gary, the frog who had escaped the zoo, said, "The spider brought us here and said that you would help us."

The frog said back, "You have to get on the bus from here and get off when you get to a place that has two trees. When you get off, you'll have to go down the pathway and you will see a tunnel with a security guard in front of it. Say the password and he will let you in. Your parents will be waiting for you!"

With the frog's instructions, they went on the bus and stayed on it for about ten minutes before they saw the two trees. They asked the driver to let them off and he did. The animals followed the pathway until they got to the tunnel with the security guard. They said, "mission control."

The guard looked at them and said, "access granted." He moved aside and let them in.

The animals went inside and saw their parents. The parents said to their children that they were so proud of them being able to escape the zoo and make it all the way back to them. They hugged each other and left to go back home where they would live happily ever after.

The Messiest Room in the Whole World

By: Julia

It was time to go home for the monsters. The portal opened. Slick-Slime-Sam, he was just called Sam for short, asked his mum if he can go and get a sock quickly.

His mum said, "No. We need to go home."

Sam didn't listen to mum. He ran as quick as he could to get a sock because he wanted a sock more than anything else! While he was going for the sock, the portal started to close. Sam thought he could make it; he was a fast runner after all. He ran as quick as he could, but it was too late. Sam was stuck!

Some time passed and the child woke up. Sam had to

hide somewhere. Sam hid in the drawer but the child needed underwear so he hid in the closet but the child needed clothes so Sam hid under the bed.

The child left some of her clothes under the bed so she looked under the bed. "Who are you?" she said when she saw the monster there.

"I'm a small, tiny monster. My name is Sam," the monster said to the child,

"You're a monster!? I thought that monsters were not real. You will be my pet?" she asked.

"Nooo! I have to go to the portal and back home." Sam replied.

"You're going nowhere!" said the girl to the monster and she closed her bedroom door and locked it! The child went to school, and Sam needed to think how he will get back home because he was very hungry and the food that the girl had in her room was disgusting.

He went to search some nasties – something that would be tasty to a monster. But, there were no nasties. Without some nasties, he will die from hunger … forever! Sam started to feel sick because without nasties he won't live.

Some time passed and the child came back home. She ran up the stairs to see her new pet. They played for a while and eventually it was time for bed.

"Good night," she said to Sam.

"I won't sleep You can't keep me here forever!" Sam said angrily.

"Why?" she said, "You're not tired today?" replied the girl. It didn't matter to her though, she was tired so she went to sleep.

Sam sat there with his arms crossed. He was annoyed. And then, he heard it. A noise behind him! It was the portal to home. Mum was here to rescue him!

"I love you!" said Sam.

"I love you too!" his mum said back.

"Let's go home," replied Sam.

"Okay," said his mum as she picked him up in a big hug.

They Lived Happily Ever After.

Drago and the Savannah

By: Arbion

This adventure starts in the jungle were Drago was getting chased by a tiger all around in a circle again and again and again until some vultures saw him and led the way back home to the Savannah.

When they arrived, the vultures wanted leftovers of kangaroo meat because they were hungry. Once they ate it all up, they left. Drago told his mum all about the tiger that tried to eat him and how the vultures saved his life by bringing him back home.

His mum was so thankful the vultures that saved him that she decided every time they come around, they can have any meat they want when they were hungry.

Some time passed and Drago decided that he was going

to go on another adventure. His mum said, "This time we're coming with you!" Therefore, they all went to the jungle but they were feeling light-headed so one sibling fainted.

While they were exploring, a snake strangled the sibling which had passed out.

"Hssssssssssss. I'm Slither the snake and if you desire to strike at me, I will, CRUSH HIS HEAD!"

Drago wasn't about to let his sibling get crushed so he pounced at Slither trying to deliver a knockout blow to the head, but the snake was too fast and crushed Drago's sibling's head.

"Noooooo!" Drago cried in desperation.

After that treacherous, long and exhausting day, mum and Drago returned home and went to bed but the dad was on patrol. The next day, they all woke up and the dad was missing so Drago and mum went to look for him and the mum found a pool of blood. So she covered it in grass.

A day passed and Drago and his mum were feeling woosy and doosy but they still needed to go further. A few hours later, they were starving so they ate some fish that they caught from a river. When they were exploring, Drago got his legs stuck in a vine of poison ivy. He cried in pain and shouted "OWEEEEE, mum!"

The cries caught the attention of his mum so she ran to him and clawed the ivy off his legs. After a few hours, they saw a piece of the Savannah and rushed strait to it but because Drago got stuck in the ivy, his legs felt numb and he couldn't run.

They were slowly making their way back and then then they saw it. There were lions in their path, in their path to freedom. Those bloodthirsty maniacs stood there with a menacing grin until Drago moved and pounced with a fierce bite in the neck of one of the beasts.

But the lions were stronger and once attacked, they attacked back. They attacked and attacked and attacked until all the hyenas were slaughtered.

The End.

Best Friends on an Island

By: Leonardo

Jerry had been transported to an island by bad people. Berry has been transported to a cave on the same island. They are both best of friends. It took them a while, but then eventually found each other on the island.

They both could see a pig and a knife. So Berry grabbed the knife and then he killed the pig to make sure that they had enough food to eat. Jerry made a fire with his lighter to cook the pig that Berry had killed. They ate the pig and went to sleep.

The next day, Jerry woke up and saw some coconuts in a tree. When he went to get them, he fell out of the tree, hit his head and passed out.

Berry woke up a bit later and saw that his friend was

passed out. Berry picked up Jerry and threw him into the water to wake him up. It worked!

Jerry screamed, "Hey! Why did you do that?!"

Berry was angry with Jerry and said, "Why on Earth did you climb that tree?!"

Jerry responded and said, "I was thirsty and wanted to drink some coconut water. Here, I even got one for you! We only have eight coconuts left, so we need to find some other water to drink because we can't drink salt water."

They dug a hole on the island to make a well and find some fresh water. It took them a while to dig it, but they eventually found water that was safe to drink. Then, they saw that there were some other animals on the island to eat. They saw two cows, one pig, three sheep, and one dog. But both Jerry and Berry agreed that they will not eat the dog.

They were hungry from all the digging, so they killed the cow, cut it up and cooked it over a fire. When it was ready, they ate as much as they could.

They were thirsty from all of the digging, so they thought they saw a boat on the beach but it wasn't actually one. It was their dog swimming in the ocean. They went to drink some water because they knew they needed it.

The next day, they see their dog sleeping and they think that he is dead. So they dig a hole to bury the dog but the dog starts barking and he jumps out of the hole. Jerry and Berry give him food to eat and name him Leo. The dog brought back some fish and they cooked it up for dinner and ate it with coconut water.

They started to eat some coconut meat and when they were done, they went for a swim. Berry found out that couldn't swim so Jerry and Leo tried to get him out and they were successful. They saved him from drowning, but Jerry had to give Berry CPR because he was not breathing. When Berry was breathing again, Jerry for a swim while Berry stayed with Leo.

Berry was playing with Leo and Leo learned some new tricks. He learned to sit, lay down, fetch and to sleep - something that he already knew.

The next day, Jerry was putting up his clothes to dry on the tree and they went to explore a cave on the island. They saw loads and loads and loads of food.

"Hurray!" they said together when they saw all the food. But it turned out that their eyes were playing tricks on them in the dark and it was actually only five pieces of bread and five bottles of water. They were still happy to have something. They took the food out of the cave.

Later in the day, Jerry taught Berry how to swim and they played chase in the water. When they finished playing, they ate and drank.

The next day, they woke up to see a boat on the beach. They screamed as loud as they could and the boat came to get them and take them back home where they lived happily ever after and shared their story with the world.

Unstoppable Girl

By: Maida

This story begins in a small barn at the stroke of midnight with a girl's dad trying to get her to steal from a palace.

"No dad, I can't I'll be in trouble and maybe die!" Cammy said as she carried a big bag of hay.

"Please, I'll try to get you a cat?" Cammy's dad said, trying to bribe her into doing something she didn't really want to do.

"No. I'm not doing it. Go sleep now, okay?" Cammy said as she kissed her dad and curled up to go to sleep.

The next morning, Cammy woke up to the sound of her dad shouting. It turns out that Cammy woke up really late and didn't do most of her jobs. Her dad screamed at her and got really mad.

"Sorry, I'll do anything to make it up to you!" Cammy said, "Please just calm down, dad. Just calm down, please!"

"Go steal at the palace and I'm not taking no for an answer this time, Cammy. You didn't do your chores and you say you'll do anything to make it up for me. So do it. Off to the palace to steal." Cammy's dad said.

"Fine!" Cammy said as she reluctantly agreed, stomping her feet.

Cammy's long blonde hair was put into a high ponytail and she was wearing a black long sleeved top, a black mask and black socks (no shoes though because her and her dad were poor) and a black small bag to put the treasure in.

"Stay safe, okay?" Cammy's dad said as he gave her a map. "Make sure you come back with something good too!"

"I know, bye!" Cammy screamed as she left.

The map was really confusing but she found her way and WHOA was this palace big. It was like Cammy's barn but like a hundred of them. And of course guards were there. Luckily, Cammy packed a smoke bomb so she used that and put it under the guards sneakily.

"Ah! This smoke! Nathaniel, press the red button. I think someone is trying to sneak in!" said one of the guards in a British accent.

"Okay, Henry!" said the other guard in a British accent too.

"Perfect!" Cammy said as she sneaked in.

The palace was very big and didn't even know where the valuables were but she eventually found some and hid fifteen different things in her bag. She was sure that it her dad could sell it for like £15,000. She was feeling quite proud of herself but then, she saw someone.

"Who are you and why are you putting my expensive stuff into your bag?" said a boy in another British accent.

"Okay, is it just me or does everybody here have a British accent?" Cammy said as she scratched her head.

"I'm sorry but you didn't answer my question," the boy said.

"Sorry, I'm poor and…"

"It's fine. Now go please."

"Huh?"

"Go and never come back."

Cammy was really confused that she didn't come back home beaten black and blue by the castle guards. She was glad she got the valuables and got out alive. Cammy and her dad used the money to get a better house and to get everything they wanted.

Everything was good until the money ran out and Cammy's dad told her to go back for more … something she was told to never do.

The Two Monsters and One Girl

By: Melisa

It was time for Olivia to go to bed but she forgot to close the window in her bedroom even though her mum reminds her to do this every single night. She got in her pj's and went to bed, snoring. When she was fully asleep, a little monster and its mother flew inside Olivia's room, right through that window she was told to keep shut.

Olivia was having a good sleep filled with good dreams. So good that she twisted and fell out of her bed! She got up, saw that her clock said midnight and went to close the window that she left open because it was cold. She curled back into bed, not noticing the monsters that were in her room.

The monsters were there looking for nasties.

"MAMA! MAMA! I- I- I smell nasty underwear!" said the little monster named Gob.

"Ok,"said the mother monster then they both wnet under the bed and found all the nasties and laid on the dirty clothes. Monsters love to lay in dirty clothes!

The next day, Olivia woke up and got dressed for school. She accidentally kicked her books under the bed so Olivia looked   under   the   bed   and   screamed!

"AHHHHHH! M-M-MONSTERS!"

Olivia's mum ran upstairs and said, "Are you alright Olivia! You are screaming."

"I saw a monster under my bed. It's under there!" Olivia said, pointing towards her bed.

"Let me check then, Olivia." Her mum crouched down

and looked under the bed. "There is nothing here, Olivia. You're being dramatic. Now get going to school, or you'll be late and will get a detention."

Olivia sighed, thinking that the monsters were maybe a dream and ran to school. She said to herself, "Were the monsters real? I don't know … I'll just do my maths work and forget about that weird dream."

After her six hour school day, the bell rang and Olivia ran home again and started looking for the two monsters. She convinced herself that it wasn't a dream and that they were really there. She was going to find them!

And she did!

"I knew you were real!" She chased the monsters around her room and caught them and put them into her hamster cage. "There! Now, when I see my mum tomorrow morning, she'll know I wasn't crazy for screaming so loudly and telling her that there were monsters under my bed!"

The monsters said nothing and just stared at her until she fell asleep.

When Olivia fell asleep, the two monsters tried to find a way out of their cage. The mother monster found a long stick and manged to get the key that was on the dresser next to them. They used the key to get out of the cage, opened the window and ran away with all of the dirty nasty clothes they found under the bed.

Olivia woke up the next working and saw that the

monsters were gone and that her window was opened. She shrugged her shoulders and said, "Weird, maybe it was a dream. Hey! Where did my dirty laundry go?"

"Oh well, I guess mum cleaned it last night when I slept. I should go downstairs to eat my breakfast and go to school."

Another Three Little Pigs

By: Neymar

Once upon a time, there were three little pigs. The three little pigs, they were going to make three houses. The little one made a house out of straw. The next pig made a house out of sticks. The last one made their house out of bricks.

There was a wolf that was coming to the little pigs. He wanted to rob their houses because there was food in the little pig's houses.

The wolf came to the first pig's house and he ate the house. The little pig ran to his friend's house that was made out of sticks.

The wolf, he followed the little and ran to where the pig was hiding. The wolf then ate the house and the three pigs ran to their final friend's house.

Then the wolf followed them and tried to eat the house made of bricks because the bricks hurt his teeth. So he tried to get in through the window but that didn't work. So he went through the chimney and the pigs ran away because the wolf wanted to eat them.

The pigs ran back home to their mum and the wolf couldn't find them.

The End

The Giant

By: Patrica

The giant was trying to get people from the water and he fell into the water. SPLASH! Fish were splashing the giant and he got angry so he went home.

He decided that he wanted to try taking over the world. The giant started eating people and that's how she got so big.

The problem is that he can not eat people because it is the worst thing ever and everyone will have died if he eats them.

I went up to the giant and said, "I think that there is some more fish in the water. My giant sweetheart, you should eat the sharks instead of the fish. Ok?"

The giant was still eating people so I said, "My sweetie,

you should really stop doing that."

The giant looked at me and said, "Want me to get angry at you? You wouldn't want that would you?"

"No!" I said. "But you need to listen to me."

He said, "Ok."

I told him, "You have to stop please and thank you. You need to promised that you are not going to do that anymore."

He said, "I promise you I won't anymore, ok."

I said to him, "I have surprise for you. Did you know my sweetheart? And you're so good now and you are so calm. You are so good now and you are surprised but you have to be like this for a long, long time."

You got it my sweety and I hope you are going to be nice at home alone and I hope you will good and I will be back. I hope you will be good and I will be good and buy something as well and I will buy a teddy bear and anything else and you have to be hiding because I am going to count up to twenty ok?

I am coming now. On the way over there she fell into some   poop   and   that   was   so   disgusting.

The Monsters Lonely Disaster!

By: Ponam

It all starts at 12am exactly, not even one second later. At this time of the day, all the windows open to let in all the monsters. These monsters are a type that likes clean houses so they can mess it up on their own because they love messes. But if the house is already messy, they will make it even worse or they will leave it but that never happened. The monsters called themselves the house disaster.

The youngest monster named Phillip said, "Look over theerre! Scissoors! Let's use the scissoorss to cut up their curtains and the bed sheets so they are uncomfortable when they go to sleep."

The older monster said, "Goood ideeaa! Let's do the entire house including the sofa's pillows and stab the sofa's as well or maybe not the sofa. Who cares! Let's just break stuff!"

Then they found all the cups and plates and hid some in the shed and even broke some so they put all the broken pieces back in the cupboard. Next, they found the guinea pig cage and saw the bag of food next to the cage and dumped all the food out and made food angels-monsters in it and they did it on the carpet because they thought it would be impossible to get the food out. But they still had a lot of more things to do like destroying the TV.

After they had finished destroying the house, which looked like a disaster, it was 6am which was the time the windows open and the portals to lead them back home. The older monster Asriel jumped through the window went into the portal back home but little did he know he left his brother in the kid's house. The journey wasn't long so he didn't think much about it because all he could think about was breakfast waiting at home.

Once Asriel got home, they all sat at the dinner table.

The mum monster asked Asreil, "Where is Phillip?"

Asreil realized he left Phillip at the kid's house, leaving him to eat dirty underwear as his breakfast.

Asreil, worried, said, "I muuust've foorgoot him ..."

Asreil ran straight from the table and went into the portal. While Asreil was in the portal Phillip noticed that his brother was gone and started saying, "Brother!? Brother!?" And with his loudest voice he screamed, "BROTHER!?"

He woke up everybody in the house. And the boy got out of the bed and ran to his parents and the monster slid under the bed. The boy said, "I think there is a monster under my bed."

After the boy named Luceth told his parents, they did not believe him but Luceth kept begging his parents to check under his bed and after fifteen minutes of begging, his parents they finally went to check because they were so annoyed. When they checked, there was nothing there under the bed because Phillip ran and hid in the box of balls. The parents were so angry because the boy annoyed them for fifteen minutes so they all went down to make coffee to relieve there stress.

But when they went down they saw that the guinea pig

food was all on the ground and the parents told Luceth to vacuum all this up. The parents went into the kitchen to make there coffee and when they opened the cupboard they saw that all the cups and plates were broken and now they were extremely angry that they told the boy he had to walk to school instead of getting a drive.

While the boy was changing he thought of an idea to set up the cage to lure the monster which he thought was under his bed and he also put guinea pig poo in the cage because it looked like chocolate. The left for school and the parents left for work.

Once the monster saw the cage and the chocolate poo , it was too good to resist so the monster stepped on the cage and the cage shut close and the monster was trapped. After the parents had finished work, they saw that their son wasn't lying because there was a monster.

After three hours, the parents went to go and pick up Luceth. When the boy saw his parents, he ran straight to his parents and gave them a hug and said, "Sorry."

The parents hugged him back and said, "We are actually sorry too."

The boy asked, "Why?"

"We will tell you at home."

"Okay."

When they all got home, the parents showed why they were sorry and the boy said, "There was a monster under my bed! I knew I wasn't lying!"

They all laughed. They all also looked after the monster because they realized it was just a kid and wasn't harmful. But the monster still did eat the guinea pig poo but nothing happened to him. It was now time for bed and they had dinner.

Now it was 12pm and the monster's brother came to rescue Phillip. He got him out of the cage while the boy and his parents slept and went back home to see their mother.

Monster Mayhem

By: Raaham

You see every child is scared of monsters and their mums just say monsters don't exist. But let me tell you a story. It starts in a little girl's room. You see, she has so many sweets. She even used M&M's as bricks to make a photo frame and melted chocolate as glue!

One day, a monster family thought they were going to have a feast at what they called Monster Mayhem. They used a portal that came not a second before and not a second after midnight and it closes an hour after it has opened.

When they entered the portal, they ended up in the little girl's room. The child monster said, "Can I have that M&M's frame please?"

"OK, fine but you have to stay with me or you'll get lost," his mum told him.

"OK!"

Then, the child got stuck! The melted chocolate was as sticky as glue! He was the one controlling the portal and he was stuck therefore he couldn't do anything.

"Help! Help!!!" the little monster yelled.

"Did someone say help?" his mum replied.

"Yes, help! Please! I'm stuck in this chocolate glue!"

"Where are you? Oh yes in the chocolate."

Then, the mother's mum ate it all and the child was free but the portal button was broken because of the stickiness.

"Oh no!" they both said as they looked at the portal button.

"We have to eat all the remaining chocolate," the child suggested, looking up at his mum.

"Let's do what we have to do," his mum nodded at him in agreement.

They ate and they ate. They licked and they licked and then it started to work. Then, it started to open up the portal!

"Yes it worked!" they both jumped for joy together.

"No time to waste it could close anytime," mum warned her little one. They ran as fast as they could and dived through the portal.

"Phew! We made it!" the little one said to his mum.

And they all lived peacefully after that, at least until next year's Monster Mayhem

The End

An Alien Meets a Human

By: Rebeka

Chapter 1

It was the morning and a little girl called Kriss, who is a five year old girl, was waking up from her sleep. It was Saturday and she was going to the park that afternoon as her mum had promised her that they would go.

Kriss went down stairs to brush her teeth and eat breakfast. "Good morning, mummy!" she said, bright and full of cheer.

"Good morning, my little raspberry cupcake!" said her mum, also known as Linda, though Kriss would never call her this because what kind of child calls their parents by their first names!

Kriss also had a bigger sister named Crystal, who

usually does nothing except sleeping in bed and texting her boyfriend or shall I say, annoying boyfriend! I mean, that's what her sister calls him.

Well, anyway, Kriss went to eat her breakfast.

munch ... munch ... munch

"Yum!!" Kriss said excitedly, "I love waffles and berriers! Thank you mum."

"Glad you like it," her mum said back with a big smile. "I know you're waiting to go to the park. We'll leave in a couple hours, ok?"

Kriss was waiting for a couple hours and now she was jumping on walls and off walls she was so exited to go to the park, especially today because the funfair was here. Crystal was not excited. The only reason she came was because her mum forced her and the fact that her boyfriend was coming as well.

Chapter 2

Crystal really didn't want to go but she needed to get some fresh air after Covid, or at least that's what her mum kept telling her. Really, the only reason she went was to meet her boyfriend.

When they arrived, Kriss asked if she could go on the Crab Ride. Her mum said sure and gave her the one pound it cost. Her mum walked away, looking at other things and Crystal was too busy hanging off her boyfriend somewhere to noticed when Kriss was getting on the ride something went wrong. While she was starting to buckle up, she blacked out and no one knew.

Chapter 3:
While she was blacked out, Kriss felt like she was in space, but a weird one. It was just like what she imagined space to look like. Maybe not the space you see in a science

textbook, but space as Kriss imagined it. There was a beach, palm trees, shops and aliens walking around.

One of the alien beetles came up to her and asked, "Beep boop bop beep bloop?"

Kriss was confused so all she could say was, "You're so cute!!!"

An alien flew down to her and said, "Hey! You're a human! What are ya doing here?"

Kriss didn't Know what to say. She just stared at the alien and started to feel ... funny.

Chapter 4:

Kriss blacked out again and when she woke up, she was in the hospital. She didn't know what happened. Her sister was crying or probably fake crying Kriss thought.

And then these men in black suits came into the room. They took Kriss to a secret room and asked tons off questions about what had happened. Kriss didn't know what to say. She thought it was all a dream.

The Wrong Room

By: Ubaydah

This story begins at midnight with a slurp and pop! A portal opened. A portal that allows monsters to go to a disgusting child's room. Or at least that's where the portal normally took monsters. But this time was different. This room was clean and it belonged to a thirteen year old, not a dirty child!

Sadly the portals have not been working well and monsters keep ending up in a neat rooms instead of dirty ones. And this family of monsters were no different.

"Mama, this room is clean. We can't eat here! What are we going to do? If we don't eat ... I'm hungry. I'm starving. I want food!"

That was Messy Jesse. The youngest monster in the

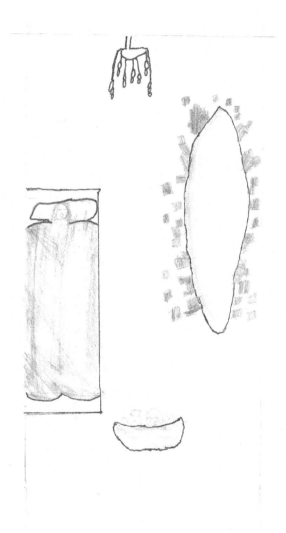

family.

They looked through the bins and tiny holes but there was nothing, absolutely nothing. What kind of teenager kept things this clean!?

"Mama, can you get this off me please?" the little one said.

"Messy Jesse, what have you done?" his mum scolded him.

"Well, I was snooping around and it clipped onto me."

She took off the mouse trap and tip toed to the washing basket.

"Jesse, come here! There are some sweaty socks from sports day at the bottom."

They sniffed the washing and sucked out all the sweat.

All of a sudden the portal opened and mum ran right in without even thinking and then slurp the portal closed.

"Mama, I swam in a washing basket! The dirty clothes were soooo good! Mama? Mama!?" The little one looked around for his mum, but he couldn't see her. All he could see was the disgustingly clean room all around him. "Mama where are you? I want my mama!"

The sound woke the sleeping girl up, plus it was morning anyway. "Who screamed mama?" said the girl and without hesitation she ran to the bathroom and got ready whilst thinking about Scooby Doo. She knew there was a monster in her room, so she was going to trap it in a cage. She hid the cage in a laundry basket with socks of course to get the monster's attention.

Jesse smelt the socks and started gobbling each of them but when she got to the last sock in the cage the door shut and Messy Jesse was stuck. The girl's trap had worked. Of course it did though, this wasn't the first monster that the girl had caught. That's what the mouse traps were for.

She picked up the cage and put it in her closet with all of the other monsters in cages. Some alive, some not so alive. And some well … let's not speak about that.

At midnight the girl went to bed and Jesse hoped that his mama would come and save him. But his mama didn't come and Jesse didn't know why. Maybe the portals were working again and this room was too clean?

"Why mama, why?" Time passed and no one came for Messy Jesse and pretty soon, she ended up like the other monsters in the cages in the girl's closet.

The Butterfly Dimension

By: Venti

Agent Jones and Renegade raider were in their office. Renegade raider said to Jones, "can you make a portal?"

Jones said, "Yes of course," and Renegade raider said, "Thank you!"

Six hours later, "Hello Renegade raider I am done, let's see if it's done," said, Renegade raider.

"Oh no the teleport thing exploded. I am so sorry," said agent Jones.

"It's okay it doesn't matter that much, I just wanted you to make me the portal is working. When you were in your office, I got a call from Doctor Slone and she said, 'Hello stupid Renegade raider I am in the butterfly dimension ha ha ha bye bye! I will see you in the butterfly dimension.'"

"Okay I've enough from Doctor Slone she will regret what she said. We need to stop her, Agent Jones can you rebuild the teleport thing."

Eight hours later, "Hello Renegade raider I am done I did everything I checked if it was okay. Let's stop Doctor Slone! Maybe she has another bad guy ... hmmm let me think. Oh I know, maybe gunner because he is a bad guy as well."

"Let's find out!"

"Oh hello Doctor Slone and gunner."

"Oh hello nice to meet you."

"Stop pretending to be nice!"

"Oh I'm not pretending to be nice!"

"Okay then what is that on your hand? Oh it's a remote. What does it do?"

"This remote will destroy the whole butterfly dimension!"

"Oh no what do we do Agent Jones?"

"I know let's pretend that we will team up with them."

They teamed up with Doctor Slone and it was tricking her. They were worried that she might try to erase their memories, so they had to work fast. They broke her machine and ran for the portal before Doctor Slone and gunner could catch up.

They jumped through the portal and made it safe. Doctor Slone and gunner were now trapped in the butterfly dimension.

THE END

Fire at the Supermarket

By: Mr Marsden

"KEVIN! WHERE ARE YOU?" Kevin was hiding.

"KEVIN!! If you don't come here right now, I'm taking away your Playstation. Kevin was crouching behind a tower of toilet rolls as his mum was shopping at the biggest supermarket in town, Fresh Extra. As soon as Kevin heard the threat about the Playstation, he burst through the tower of toilet rolls and ran back to his mum's side. "Now put your hand on the twins' buggy handle and don't let go."

Kevin was a hyperactive boy. He never walked anywhere when he could be running and he found it very difficult to sit still. Kevin had dark brown, wavy hair though you wouldn't know it to look at him. Last year, Mum had to shave his head when he got chewing gum stuck in his hair and it was just easier to keep it shaved, Kevin's trainers were always coming off when he ran. He couldn't tie laces so Mum bought him velcro trainers, but that didn't work either since he got them covered in thick mud last week. Kevin was a scruffy boy.

As they walked down the biscuit aisle, Kevin recognised all the usual supermarket noises. Mums chatting, babies crying, trolleys crashing and checkouts beeping and whirring. He looked over at the customers putting their shopping on the checkout conveyor belt - it reminded him of the running machines at the gym near his school. It was the only time Kevin stopped running, so he could watch all the grown-ups sweating and gasping on the running machines.

"How fast could I run on that checkout?" Kevin wondered.

"Come on, Kevin." Mum yanked his arm. "We need to go to the back of the store to get a fresh baguette.

Mum started marching towards the in-store bakery and pulled Kevin along with her. Kevin loved the smell of freshly-baked bread. He noticed it was coming from a door marked STAFF ONLY but he didn't know what that meant. Kevin's mum moved away from the buggy to pick up a baguette. As soon as she looked away, Kevin ran through the door and was gone.

"I'll just close my eyes for two minutes whilst I hide from Mum," Kevin thought before sitting down behind the door to the bakery. When he woke up, everything was dark.

Kevin panicked. He didn't like the dark so he sprinted through the bakery doors and found that the supermarket aisles were lit better than the bakery, but not by very much. Bright lights were shining near the store entrance. Kevin jogged nervously towards the light and soon found himself in the vegetable aisle.

Giant baking potatoes were stacked into a pyramid-shape like a volcano of vegetables. Kevin grabbed one from the bottom and the volcano erupted covering him in a lava flow of potatoes. "That hurt," thought Kevin. He saw a sign for SOFT FRUITS and shouted, "That should be safer!" He sprinted towards the strawberries, slipped on a crushed grape on the floor and went crashing head-first into a box of kiwis. Kevin collected his trainer from the banana shelf (where it had landed) and ran towards the checkouts instead.

Kevin was certain that he could use one of the checkouts as a running machine. He leapt up onto the conveyor belt. Was it switched on? Kevin couldn't tell so started running anyway. But the second he started, his floppy trainer came off (as it usually did) and Kevin fell sideways onto the next till which was self-service. "UNEXPECTED ITEM IN THE BAGGING AREA," reported a robotic voice from the checkout speaker. Collecting his shoe again, Kevin noticed a small cut on his right hand and decided to go and find a plaster next. He wasn't sure where to get one, so he just set off towards the brightest lights.

All of a sudden, a siren started blaring, "NEE-NAW-NEE-NAW-NEE-NAW." Kevin couldn't believe his own eyes. He was now in the toy section, staring with his mouth wide open. It was the luxury, motorized fire truck that he had begged his parents for. He wanted it as a birthday present but his dad had said that it was far too expensive. And here it was. Bright blue lights blaring and the door open ready for someone to climb in. He reached for the handle but before he boarded, he noticed a fireman's outfit for sale just next to it. As quick as a flash, he pulled on the fireman's outfit (just like a real fireman getting ready to go to an emergency) and pulled the fire truck off the shelf and onto the shopfloor.

Kevin was in heaven. As he sat in the driver's seat. Fiddling with all the buttons and controls, he worked out how to change the siren and alarm settings. After turning everything off, he pointed the fire truck down the toy aisle and set off. Halfway down the aisle, just past all the Lego and Star Wars toys, he noticed a sign on the door in front which said FIRE EXIT. Kevin knew exactly what to do. He switched the lights and siren on, slammed his right velcro trainer down hard on the accelerator and smashed through the fire exit doors and then slammed on the brakes when he saw what was on the other side.

Kevin was overjoyed. Towering over Kevin was a

fireman, a real fireman.

"What are you up to, young man?" said the fireman.

Kevin was also terrified. Standing next to the fireman was Kevin's Mum.

"KEVIN!! Just you wait until we get home."

One week later, Kevin was reading his book about the Fire Service. The kind fireman had turned up at his door one day to give it to him as he was so interested in becoming a fireman when he was older. Kevin opened the book and put it down in the place where his Playstation usually was and continued colouring in his picture. He did miss his Playstation (for six whole months) but not as much as he thought he would.

The Garden Crab

By: Mr Bateman

Two seagulls whirled and swirled above the gardens, bickering and mewling. One of them had something in its beak. The other wanted it. As they banked and clashed the object was dislodged from the beak. It cascaded over and over in the air, bounced lightly on some overgrown grass in a wooded garden and came to rest. The seagulls screeched in fury, glaring at each other yellow-eyed, and veered away, back to the nearby sea and the richly supplied rock pools.

Zeta had landed on her legs, the whole length of which slotted neatly into the depths of the cool grass. The grass tickled her underside. Zeta swiveled her eyes around cautiously. The seaweed around her seemed very strange, terribly dry, and she could no longer hear the sound of the sea. That was alarming. She swung back her eye stalks to look up. Green seaweed stretched out above her seeming to float in mid-air. It was as if the tide was in, but also out. And no water.

She waited.

There were lots of sounds. There were high-pitched screeches, chirps and whistles coming from all around her and at all distances. They were like the gulls, but not the same. She could see fittings of movement. Yes, they had wings like the gulls but were not the same colour. There was also a seal somewhere, she noticed. She could hear the distinctive barking nearby.

This place was like the rock pool she knew, but so different as well. It was full of life. And if it was anything like the rock-pool it would be life that was hiding, moving, eating, playing…and hunting.

Was there a rock she could crawl under? When the tide was out and the rock-pools exposed, it was much less safe, especially when you didn't have your older brothers and sisters to look out for you. And she'd already escaped one mortal danger. She rotated her eyes in almost a full circle, assessing the colours and shapes, then decided to head for what could be an orange-tinted rock nearby.

At least moving through the grass made little sound, unlike the scrape and clack of the ends of her legs on the rocks. The sound that had caught the gull's attention earlier. This new rock was smooth, jagged-edged and amazingly it was hollow, like a small cave. She sneaked into the shade of the hollow and turned around so that she could look out of the entrance, her back to the damp wall of the cave. And waited.

As her eyes adjusted to the dim light, she noticed that there were small round rocks attached to the inside of the walls. 'Could they be shellfish?' she wondered. She lifted up a claw and gave one of them a light tap. It fell straight off and clattered onto a small flat rock on the ground. A watery scream rang out.

The thing had landed on its back and revealed the tell-tale soft, meaty underside of a shellfish! Some kind of clam or whelk that lived here in this dry sea? Shellfish were notoriously impatient, Zeta knew. If they were in a dangerous situation they couldn't wait but five minutes without moving and revealing themselves. Sure enough, after just three minutes the little disc of greenish meat rippled and bubbled and a head slipped slowly out, wrinkled with scales and waving tiny feelers about. It twisted around, the wet body gripping the rock and the rounded shell righting itself.

"Who do you think you are, stranger!" piped the snail, as its feely four eyes settled on the crab. "How do you expect me to get back up there in this dry weather?"

The shellfish's accent was a bit strange, but as it was water-based, Zeta could understand it pretty well.

"I'm sorry," she said, "I'll pop you back up if you like?"

She reached out a claw to clasp the shell.

"No, no, no, no, no!" begged the snail. "Never you mind. I'll just settle here thanks. Perfectly comfy-like here on this shard of pot."

She waggled her feelers curiously at Zeta, seemingly deciding whether or not to say something.

"You're new here, aren't you?"

Zeta nodded her body.

"What..er..what happened to your shell, if you don't mind me asking? Have you been attacked?"

Zeta was confused. She'd been grabbed, but not attacked. Then she realised that the little animal may not have ever seen a crab. After all, she'd never seen a shellfish as puny as this, so maybe the shellfish had never seen something as strong as her! This made her laugh, because her shell was so weak compared to all her brothers and sisters.

"Well!" huffed the snail. "That is rude! Laughing at me when I was simply showing some concern for your..your, er.. 'badly-damaged' shell, shall we say?.."

"Oh!" said Zeta, slightly offended, but deciding to pass over it. "Sorry. I wasn't laughing at you. I did get attacked by a sea gull earlier, but no, this is how I look, and all my brothers and sisters too! These spikes and jagged edges are excellent for defence, and my shell is extremely tough. Perhaps not enough to resist a sea gull, but strong enough against other beasts!"

"Hmm, ok," said the snail, doubtfully. She seemed to make a decision, made a strange sort waggle with her feelers, and introduced herself;

"Pot-slider the Snail is my name, but you can call me just Pot-slider. Welcome to the Garden!"

Zeta smiled, wondering if she had made a friend.

"My name's Zeta. I am a Crab."

"Those sea gulls are brutes," said Pot-slider, not acknowledging Zeta's name or animal type. "One of them, Gordon, ate six of my cousins. Left their shells he did, all strewn about on the human path. I remember them so clearly; Slime-most, Rain-scarper, Wrong-direction, Zig-Zag, Big-shell and Three-antennas. Three-antennas was always out of luck. Wrong-direction wasn't much better." A tear oozed out of Pot-slider's shell.

"Don't cry," said Zeta, "You'll dry out," she added kindly, sensing again the lack of moisture around.

"What is the Garden?" Zeta then asked.

Pot-slider brightened. "Ah! The Garden! A vast land of great opportunity – food everywhere! Lush, succulent vegetation! But alas, we are a tribe in danger. The Spiked-One and the Legged-Ones hate us, they diminish our number, not to say the effect of the attacks of the Winged-Ones. It's a wonder we're here at all. Mind you, with my leadership here in Pot Home, we plan to strike back! Wait for the rain, my friend, then, in a dark night we shall surge forth from our base, all of us in our reduced multitudes, and eat! Oh we shall eat and eat and eat! Then, enemies, you will see us in our millions, sucking and gorging on the land 'til not one leaf remains!"

Pot slider had fallen into a sort of reverie, something Zeta had seen before in shellfish, despite her few months of life, and so waited until the animal had finished, exhausted, and fallen back to sleep.

'Could the Garden be a land of opportunity for Zeta too?' she thought. If it was vast, how would she get back to the sea? The enormity of the situation was coming home to her and she felt unsafe and alone again, despite being surrounded by shell-fish Snails.

Zeta waited. She was hungry. She was thirsty. What could she eat? What would her friend taste like? It didn't seem fair to eat your friend, or even your friend's friends. And how would that impact on the 'surging forth' during the rain? Rain would be great, thought Zeta. Rain softened the rock-pool water when the tide was out. Rain danced and sang on your back.

Life had to live, thought Zeta, even if it got eaten itself, and so ended life. She stepped out of Pot Home and back into the tall strands of somehow floating seaweed, swivelling her eyes and body carefully and stopping when the Winged-Ones flew over. Her crab senses smelled food, deeper in the foliage. Flies led her to it, and the smell was overpowering. How her mouth watered! She batted away the flies and bent her body in, her mouth parts working furiously in the soupy mush. Quite what the animal had been, she did not know, but eating it had come naturally. As her favourite brother Gamma always said; 'Do what you are led to do.'

A slow movement caught her eye. She raised her body up. Another snail gliding along. It was moist and shaded in this corner of the garden, Snails could be on the move here. The snail wanted to share the meal but its eyes hadn't picked out the crab. Then Zeta saw two more eyes, staring straight at her through the leaves. Bulgy eyes like another crab, eyes on top of the head like another crab, its size similar to hers, a newish crab. But it was green, had no shell, and was shiny smooth.

They both froze as the snail drew closer between them, their eyes locked together, sizing each other up. The snail drew nearer. The eyes locked tighter. Zeta could see the beating of the heart of the beast opposite by the fluctuation of the skin. A critical moment was approaching. The snail slid right between them, reaching the pool of food. The beast's eyes slid away from Zeta to the snail and BANG! It leapt, wrenched the snail up in a whip-like tongue and immense gaping mouth, elongated its body like a sea-snake and jumped crashing away over a clump of seaweed and...SPLASHED somewhere!!

A short scamper away, there was a shrieking and shouting of about 20 voices with one voice ringing back out tauntingly towards her;

"Loser! Eat grass, Spikey-Head!"

There was more splashing.

"Move over, Flipper!"

"Get your elbow out of my face, Bulge-eye!"

"That is my knee, Triple-joint! Oi, I was going to catch that fly!"

"Sharing is caring, Green-rope!"

Zeta thought they sounded like her own brothers and sisters, brawling, joking and larking about. She determined to get a closer look and crept through the foliage towards the sound. The seaweed parted around a square rock-pool! Several rounded heads with the same bulging eyes floated on the surface. And more of the smooth beasts sat around, their bodies folded up into ball shapes, on logs and rocks that seemed to have been arranged around the outside of the pool. Instead of building rock towers, as the crabs did, their game seemed to be flicking out their tongues like whips to make loud cracking sounds, flicking each other behind the head, or using them to catch whatever type of small flying animal dared pass overhead. They seemed to have voracious appetites, which explained why their bodies were so rounded.

"Eeww!" said one of the Legged-Ones, it's Spikey-head. It moves SIDEWAYS!!"

The Legged-ones hooted with laughter as they saw Zeta

approach.

"That is so funny!" they screamed with laughter, several of them falling off the log that was positioned across the pool. One of them rolled off a large leaf of seaweed that rested on the pond surface.

Zeta decided to ignore them. Sideways was the way she moved. It was the way every crab moved in the rock-pool and sideways was the way every crab she had ever seen moved, and it was perfectly good enough for her. She nonchalantly picked her way to the edge of the pool, and to the astonishment of all the Legged-Ones, slipped into the water!

It was murky, warm and not at all salty. But at least it was water, and Zeta was able to float luxuriously and fill her shell gaps with the soft nourishing water.

"Hey, but we live here!" bubbled the Legged-Ones, "You can't stay here, you'll scratch us and pinch us. Scuttle off sideways, won't you?"

"I am here, so I am here!" said Zeta, thinking it was something Gamma might have said.

"Eww, funny accent too," said one of them.

There was a lot of huffing and puffing, shaking and splashing as many of the Legged-Ones climbed out of the rock-pool in protest. Then, strangely, everything went quiet. And stayed quiet. Soon there was a terrifying scream. Frogs splashed desperately back into the pool, diving deep and crouching behind seaweed or burying themselves in the mud at the bottom.

"Sharp-teeth has struck again," they murmured, "She's got Soft-grip. Soft-grip is dead!" they sobbed.

"You ran away, Flash-tongue," spat Blue-lips, Soft-grip's father, "You said you loved her!"

Flash-tongue nuzzled deeper in the mud, whimpering.

"What's happened? Who's Sharp-teeth?" asked Zeta.

"Oh, you're all right, aren't you, Spikey-head? <u>You'll</u> never get eaten with that back on you."

"Maybe I can help?"

The Legged-Ones turned their backs on her, one or two floated to the surface to scan the garden, just the very tops of their eyes breaking through the water surface like static bubbles. They could hear the excruciating sound of Sharp-teeth feeding.

Zeta spent the next few days in an uneasy truce with the Legged-Ones, who at least told her that they were known as 'Frogs' to each other. She met a 'Toad' as well. She was able to go back and forth in the garden and managed to cope ok, trying different food, sometimes eating insects that happened by. It was instinct. The thing would scamper past and – whip – just like a frog tongue, into the mouth.

One day she met the Land Urchin; Old-Spikey. A big wet nose leaned down and sniffed at her from high above. Zeta rose up her claws in defence and defiance.

"Nice back!" said the giant. "The spikes need a bit of

work, but, well, keep going, you'll get there, little one." And it shuffled off on four great stumpy legs in search of Snails or 'Slugs'.

At the end of the third week, Zeta was confused to hear cracking noises coming from her shell. Then she remembered, from watching her older brothers and sisters; her shell was going to disintegrate. When it fell apart she would have to climb out quickly, drink great quantities of water to swell up, and then hide somewhere. Then her new shell that was forming underneath would expand and harden. She would have grown bigger, all in one go.

The Frogs had grown less haughty and had stopped ganging up on her. Some of the little ones had even taken to sitting on her back and enjoyed getting bumpy sideways rides. The older frogs were appreciative of Zeta, to them it was childcare. The little Frogs could position their little bodies comfortably between the sharp parts of the shell and hold on to the spikes with their little hands. They chortled with joy at the funny rides that Zeta gave them, and Zeta warmed to the Frogs.

Zeta explained the shell process and the frogs agreed to look after her while she went through the changes. When Zeta finally emerged from the pond a few days later she was much bigger and stronger. And now she had some ideas about this garden and its occupants. She had had the time to think about life in the rock-pools back home and she thought she could help with the life in the Garden.

First, she dragged lots of broken pots together from all corners of the Garden (which she had discovered was not as vast as had been previously mentioned). She made Pot Home into Pot City for the Snails. She climbed the seaweed and knotted leaves together to make a giant shady seaweed patch to keep the city moist. She dug a small trench so that overflow water from the rock pool fed into the city.

This delighted the Snails as they could build up their army in just the right conditions. And it delighted the Frogs, as the small army expeditionary forces could be snapped up and eaten.

For the Frogs, Zeta used her strength to build several defensive towers around the pool. These shielded the Frogs from attacks by Sharp-teeth, where they could gather and whip out their tongues at him to tease and confuse whenever he came slinking by. Of course, Sharp-teeth was an excellent hunter, and any foraging Frog was still not safe, but at least Home Pool was now safe.

And so, Zeta was accepted by the Garden animals and even liked. And then, one day, the gulls came back.

Zeta was stretching out her claws into the sun on the top of Zeta's Tower, as it was now known. It was the tallest rock tower that stretched up in to the sky and it had been built so that it raised up from the very centre of the Pool. But down came the pair of gulls, raucous and determined, snatching her up and wheeling her away.

"Zeta!" her friends wailed, "Zeta, we've lost Zeta!" Their voices trailed into the distance, as the landscape swirled dizzily in Zeta's vision.

"Gotcha!" scraped Gordon's voice.

"No, Gordon, I've gottit!" and Zeta was lurched to the side as Stephen violently barged Gordon, loosening his grip, and transferring the crab to his own talons.

And so the fight went on until beneath her she saw blue. She swivelled her eyes down. The tide was receding; the rock-pools were about to rise from the sea. Zeta looked at the strong beak above her and the strong talons around her. But then she looked at her strong claws. And waited. She waited until she recognised a swirl of water circling below her, in what would soon be a large, particularly-shaped and therefore recognisable rock pool and BANG! Her claws slammed down and pincered the skinny legs of the gull.

An anguished scream!

And down she went, cascading over and over in the air, down.. down.. and SPLASH into the sea, and softly.. softly.. sinking, landing on her big legs, the tips of which dipped gently into the soft sand of a what had just now returned into rock pool. Zeta's rock pool. Home Pool.